Published in the United States by

Howell Canyon Press

5929 151st Avenue SE
Snohomish, WA 98290
888.252.0411 orders and fax
www.HowellCanyonPress.com
mail to: info@HowellCanyonPress.com

Printed in China by C&C Offset Printing

Publisher's Cataloging-in-Publication
(Provided by Quality Books, Inc.)

Howell, Trisha Adelena, 1962-
  The adventures of Melon and Turnip / story by Trisha
Adelena Howell ; illustrations by Paul Lopez.
    p.cm.
    SUMMARY: Melon and Turnip leave their garden home to
explore life. They meet an apple tree, a squirrel, a
pine tree, and other new friends on their journey of
discovery.
    ISBN 1-931-210-04-7

    1. Fruit–Juvenile fiction. 2. Vegetables–Juvenile
fiction. [1. Fruit–Fiction. 2. Vegetables–Fiction.
3. Behavior–Fiction. 4. Friendship–Fiction]
I. Lopez, Paul, ill. II. Title.
PZ7.H8383Adv 2004   [E]
                            QB104-288

Book Designer: Bonnie Bushman, 405 Ashley Court, Kalispell MT 59901

DEDICATION
For Greg Gunderson, the original turnip and a very dear friend

"I celebrate myself, and sing myself,
and what I assume, you shall assume,
for every atom belonging to me as good belongs to you."

Walt Whitman, *Song of Myself*

ACKNOWLEDGEMENTS
Paul Lopez has created fabulous illustrations for this book and for *The Princess and the Pekinese*. I am eternally grateful. Thanks to John Thompson of Illumination Arts, who has been a wonderful mentor, editing many versions of the manuscript while encouraging me and bringing joy with his sunny disposition. I am grateful as well to my mother, Frances Thomas Fike, the sharpest and most thorough editor on the planet. Dale Smith and Lisa Hauser were also outstanding—this book wouldn't have been nearly as good without their wise advice. In addition, I don't know what I would have done without the marvelous teachers and librarians who so generously perused the manuscript, making excellent suggestions. My designer, Bonnie Bushman, was very patient with me and fabulous about working under ridiculously short deadlines. Sharon Castlen of Integrated Book Marketing has been a great help with all aspects of this and my other books. Thank you all! My deepest thanks also to my beloved husband Dean, whose amazing love, support, and healing energy have filled my life with happiness and health.

We are members of Publishers in Partnership—replanting our nation's forests.

There once was a land of sunny
meadows, pine forests, and sparkling
waters. Nestled in a valley beside a
gently flowing river was a glorious
garden.

All the fruits and vegetables
growing there were strong and
healthy. The air carried the sweet
smell of flowers and the pleasant
hum of happy insects.

Two friends living in this garden paradise longed for adventure.

"Hey, Melon," Turnip called out one day. "Let's go see the world!"

Melon listened to the sounds that were carried on the wind. "I do love the songs we hear from beyond the river!"

"Then let's go!" Turnip spun his body out of the soil.

Melon's eyes grew very wide.

"What's the matter?" Turnip asked. "Are you afraid? Don't be. Just roll along till your vine snaps. You'll be fine."

Melon wasn't so sure. She'd never been without her vine before. What would happen if she broke free?

"Hey, you two!" growled a red Pepper. "How's a body to rest when you're always chattering?"

"We're leaving." Turnip turned deep purple with anger. "You can sleep when we're gone, you old stick-in-the-mud!"

Pepper strained against his stem. Steam poured out of his ears. "You're the one who lives in the mud, you dirty root!"

Turnip called the Pepper more names. The whole pepperbush shook. Each pepper glared at Turnip. After all, they were **hot** peppers.

Turnip grew impatient waiting for Melon to make up her mind. "Are we going or not?"

Trembling, Melon took a deep breath then rolled around in the soft dirt until there was a loud snap. Soon she was tumbling down the hill toward the river, with Turnip bouncing after her.

Melon splashed into the river. "What a grand parade of dancing water! Won't you join me?"

Turnip dipped his root and was surprised by how smooth and inviting the water felt. Without hesitation, he sprang in.

They were happy floating down the river, when suddenly a big crow swooped down and grabbed Melon! She slipped beneath the water to avoid its sharp claws, but the mean bird circled for another attack.

Just as the crow swooped again, Turnip pushed Melon onto the shore. He jumped from the water and hid with her in the tall grass beneath an apple tree. As hard as the bird tried, it could not find them and finally flew away.

Melon and Turnip peeked out from their hiding place and heard a song coming from the tree:

> This is the melody we sing
> Of apples: summer, fall, and spring
> Swaying and playing
> Pleased we're staying
> Welcoming the world's wonder
> We're not afraid of the bird
> Joy is our favorite word.

Turnip hummed along, until the apples stopped singing to ask, "Who are you?"

"I'm Turnip, and this is Melon. We've come to see the world and hear everyone's songs."

"Wonderful!" The apples smiled. "It's exciting to have visitors! We're so pleased you've come."

Traveling on, Melon and Turnip saw an oak tree where a happy squirrel sang as she packed nuts into a hollow:

Store the nut and seed.
Patience is what you need.
Make the dreams come true
That are worthy of you.

"Hello," Squirrel called out. "Would you like to take a nut, my dears?"

Turnip smiled. "No, thank you."

Melon rolled closer. "Are you happy working so hard?"

"Oh yes, my dear. I'll be well-fed all winter. My dream is to fill my home with nuts, and that's what I'm doing."

"We're doing what we dreamed too." Melon smiled. "We're seeing the world and discovering its songs."

Melon and Turnip kept rolling and bouncing until they heard a tall pine tree singing:

Long I've lived and much I've seen:

Winter's snowy carpet, spring's lively green.

But I can sum it up in a word or two:

Do unto others as you'd have done to you.

"Yes!" Melon smiled brightly. "I don't hurt anyone, and I don't want anyone to hurt me. I'm happier when I do things that make others happy."

Turnip nodded. "What we give away comes back to us. We're all connected to each other on the inside. Don't you think so, Mr. Pine?"

"Of course!" Pine said, lifting them high into his branches. "And I'm happy to show the world to you. Look!"

Gazing across the valley, Melon and Turnip could see their beautiful garden, the river shining like diamonds, and the tall mountains. "Thank you so much, Mr. Pine!"

"You're welcome." Pine gently set them on the ground. "I'm always glad to make others happy."

Melon and Turnip heard a
rustling nearby.
A long brown snake
slithered as he sang:

Slither and slide
Catch 'em by the head
Catch 'em by the hide
A feast is in the making
And soon they'll be shaking
As I swallow 'em alive!

"That's horrible!" Melon trembled. "How can you kill innocent creatures?"

"Everyone has to eat." Snake slithered toward her. "I respect my prey because they keep me alive. It's the cycle of life."

Melon gasped. "But you should treat others as you want to be treated. Would you want to be eaten?"

Snake paused. "If eating me were the only way another creature could survive, I'd understand. In the animal world that's the way it works. It's not personal at all.

Turnip nodded. "At least he's honest about it."

"But I don't like what he's saying!" Melon's voice shook.

"I am who I am." Snake looked straight into Melon's eyes. "I'm honest with everyone, just as I want everyone to be honest with me."

Suddenly an enormous rat sprang out, grabbed Melon, and rolled her away. Turnip shouted, "Snake, please do something!"

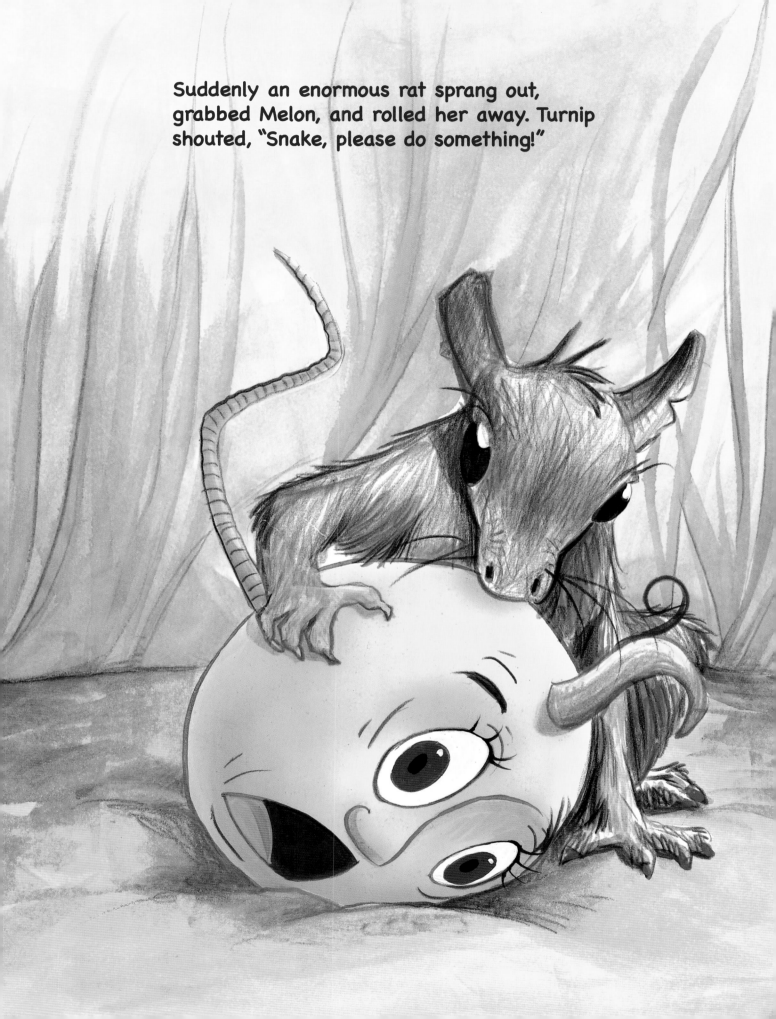

Melon screamed and squeezed her eyes shut, but not before the rodent's sharp teeth arched above her and plunged downward. She heard a gulp, and then nothing.

Melon slowly opened one eye. The rat was gone, and in its place lay Snake, licking his lips contentedly.

"Thank you. You saved my life, Snake. I'm sorry I criticized you."

"Thank you for providing my meal. That rat tasted quite good."

Melon smiled. "I won't take it personally. Now I know that it grabbed me only because it was hungry. But I'm really glad you saved me!"

After Snake slithered away
to digest his meal, the
grass beside Melon and
Turnip danced and sang.

Be happy each day,
Celebrate and play.

Follow your dreams,
Bright as sunbeams.

Treat creatures with love,
From here to above.

Be truthful with all others,
Honesty and respect are brothers.

"That's the wisest song I've ever
heard." Melon smiled with gratitude
and was inspired to sing:

I love the adventure of living,
Of receiving and of giving.
All is well with me;
I'm happy as can be.

Turnip was nodding along with the song. But then he noticed that Melon was starting to wither from being out in the sun without water. His own hard peel had also begun to shrivel, so they both made their way back to the river and slipped in.

Soon a strong wind swept through and tossed them into rocky rapids! To help Melon avoid a sharp rock, Turnip wrapped his greens around her smooth rind. Seeing a large log looming ahead, he paddled frantically with his root to avoid a collision.

Exhausted, Turnip couldn't help drifting back into the rapids when Melon, with a burst of strength, managed to roll them both out of the water and onto a sandy beach.

After catching his breath, Turnip gratefully sang:

Blessings to one and all
My anger now is small.
Joy to everyone
I think life is fun.

Upon returning to the garden, Melon and Turnip fascinated the others with tales of their adventures. They told how they learned to be joyful from the apples, to follow their dreams from Squirrel, to be kind to others from Pine, and to always be honest from Snake. But Pepper never smiled nor laughed.

Turnip turned to him. "I'm sorry I was so mean to you, Pepper. I was wrong not to respect your feelings."

Pepper's angry face relaxed into a smile. "I guess I didn't think about your feelings either. I'm sorry too."

After Melon and Turnip became friends with Pepper, all their neighbors joined in a song of celebration.

And for the rest of the summer, everyone in the garden played and sang songs together.

Dear Reader,

As you may know, a book can change a lot from its first draft to what is finally printed. Just like outtakes at the end of a movie can be fun to watch and can give you insight into the process of creating that movie, so comparing the first draft of a book with the final can give you an idea of how a book changes over time.

I wrote *The Adventures of Melon and Turnip* about three years before it was published. When it came time to actually print it, I realized that the poem songs it contained were not very accessible for children. So I simplified the words and cut the number of song lines from 59 to 36. Here, below, are the original lines.

How many differences can you find between the original and the final songs? Which lines would you have changed and which would you have kept? Why? Considering questions like these can help you to understand what it's like being a writer and also to improve your own work should you choose to be a writer yourself.

Best of luck to you in all your activities, and do write me and let me know how you liked this book!

Trisha Adelena Howell

Page 12-13: Song of the Apples

This is the song we sing
A song of apples by the spring
Swaying and playing
Pleased we're staying
Welcoming the world's wonder
We're not afraid of the bird's raid
We'll never trade the joy we've made
Even lightning and thunder
Can't rain on our parade.

Page 14-15: Squirrel's Song

Pluck the lovely nut;
Store the savory seed.
Don't slip into a rut;
Patience is what you need.
Every day is new.
And so, my dear, are you.
Work and you will see
The beauty that can be.
Every moment an adventure,
Reaping what you venture.

Page 16-17: Pine's Song

Long I've lived and much I've seen:
Winter's snowy carpet, spring's lively green.
But I can sum it all up in a word or two:
Do unto you neighbor as you'd have done to you.

Page 18-19: Snake's Song

Drimple and drither
Slither and slide
Catch 'em by the forelegs
Catch 'em by the hide
A feast is in the making
Food for the taking
Oh, how soon they'll be shaking
As I swallow them alive!

Page 24-25: Song of the Grass and Melon's Song

After Snake slithered away, Melon and Turnip felt a pleasant caress from the dancing grass. As more blades joined in, the faint whisper became a chorus:

Enter the world with wonder
Energy strong as thunder
Celebrate and play
So your spirit is king.

Work hard with ambition
To ensure your nutrition
Be active each day
So your body may sing.

Treat creatures with love
From far below to high above
You are one with all others
You receive what you give.

Grace the world with truths
Whether this vexes or soothes
Honesty and respect are brothers
The noblest way to live.

Your life never ends
Your spirit ascends
Keep singing your song
All your life long.

"That's the wisest song I've ever heard." Melon's eyes shone with gratitude. Then she found her own song inside and was inspired to sing:

I love the adventure of each day
And no longer into fear will stray
To life and death, amen
I know I'll be back again.

Page 28: Turnip's Song

Blessings to one and all
My anger now is small.
Though our danger was tall
I think life is a ball.

Dear Reader,

Sometimes because there is not enough space for the words on the page or because having them there slows down the story too much, a character has to be taken out.

Such was the case with Melon's timid friend Squash, who learned to be less afraid when she saw that Melon had returned safely from her journey. Her story—together with the other material already on the below pages—was simply too much text for a children's book, and I was unsure how much her presence actually added. So I decided to remove her.

However, you can still see Squash on pages 6 and 29, and here is her story. Do you think it was a good idea to take out Squash? Have you or your friends ever felt afraid like Squash? What did you do? When you are afraid, it is always great to have someone you know who can encourage you and make you feel better. Usually, the fear itself is worse than what you fear!

Best wishes to you,

Trisha Adelena Howell

Page 8-9

A soft whimpering caught Melon's attention. In the next row a yellow Squash was trembling under several squash leaves. Melon frowned. "Why are you crying?"

"I want to see the sun." Squash spoke just above a whisper.

Melon thought that her friend did look rather pale. "His sparkling smile awaits you out here!"

"But I might get burned and die."

"Don't be afraid; you won't die." Melon's voice was gentle and encouraging.

Turnip turned to Melon. "Are we going or not?"

Melon considered Squash, smiled then rolled in the soft dirt until there was a loud snap. As she tumbled down the hill toward the river, Turnip bounded after her.

Page 30-31

Leaves rustled as Squash peered out. "Melon?"

"Squash, I'm so happy to see you!" Melon said.

"Really?" Squash inched her head out from the under the leaves. "I was thinking that maybe if you could survive such a great adventure, I could survive seeing the sun. What do you think?"

"I think you're right."

Squash slowly pushed aside her leaves and looked up at the radiant sun. "Wow! It's so beautiful! I feel so happy."

"Because you're living your dream."

"And I'm only a little afraid."

"It's okay to be afraid." Melon said. "Just don't ever let it keep you from being yourself."

As Squash danced with Melon, and Turnip played hopscotch with Pepper, the other fruits and vegetables joined in. Everyone had fun for the rest of the summer.

Dear Reader,

The art for a children's picture book may change a lot from start to finish and requires a strong focus on detail and on consistency. In the case of *The Adventures of Melon and Turnip*, it took me over a year to create the final artwork.

First, I read the story carefully and visualized all the scenes in my mind. I tried especially to get a sense of who Melon and Turnip were and how they might look. My first attempt is below. Neither Trisha nor I were satisfied with this Melon and Turnip. They looked old and stodgy, not projecting the energy and enthusiasm that we wanted our characters to have and that the words of the story showed they had.

So Trisha and I brainstormed how we wanted our characters to look, and I did the studies below and on the opposite page to develop those ideas. As you can see, some of these look like the final Melon and Turnip and some don't. Look carefully. What differences and similarities can you see between these sketches and the artwork in the book? What do you like about the way Melon and Turnip ended up looking, and what would you have done differently? How would you approach illustrating a book such as this?

What I did, once I'd finalized all the characters, was to imagine the exact setting for each scene. As an artist, it is easy to create beautiful pictures in my mind and on paper. But as an illustrator, I had to make sure that each picture contained all the elements necessary in each scene—as well as other things not even mentioned in the words but which would make the story come alive even more. Look closely. How many little animals and other extra details can you find in the illustrations that are not talked about in the story?

Finally, it was important to make sure that all the illustrations were consistent. The first illustration in the book shows the whole scene—not only the garden where Melon and Turnip live but also the river, forests, meadows, and mountains surrounding them. If you look closely, you will see all the story locations on this two-page spread. Now look at the rest of the illustrations. Can you find where each of them is located on this first painting?

The last step is adding color. All the above steps happen when the artwork is still in the black and white drawing stage so that I can easily make changes. After all the characters, the basic scenes, the little extra details, and the consistency between scenes are finalized,

melon   Turnip

"CHARACTER DEVELOPMENT"
PAUL LOPEZ

it's time to start over, copying the drawings exactly as colorful paintings. Before I do this, however, I have to figure out which colors to use. In the case of *The Adventures of Melon and Turnip*, Trisha and I had several discussions before we decided on the exact color Melon and Turnip should be. Otherwise, the colors were easy: bright and bold watercolors were my choice for this very upbeat yet soft and emotional story.

After my artwork was completed, there was still more to do. All my paintings were scanned by a huge machine, and these scans became the computer files that the page designer worked with as well as what the printer printed from. The printer held onto the original artwork during this process so that he could make sure that the computer files printed out in the finished book in the exact colors that I used in the original artwork.

Creating illustrations (and art in general) is a great adventure—kind of like the adventures that Melon and Turnip go on here. You discover new and exciting things as well as learn a lot when you set out to bring to life in actual illustrations the imaginative vision that is in a story or in what you see when you look at our beautiful world. I hope that all of you will experience the thrill of drawing and painting. Don't worry about whether or not you have talent. The point is to experience the challenge, the sense of discovery, and the joy of putting your own unique vision onto paper, into a sculpture, or into whatever form you want to use to express yourself.

Go out and have fun with your art, whatever it may be!

Paul Lopez

Howell Canyon Press

features health-promoting and uplifting books, videos and CD-ROMS.

Available now:

The Princess and the Pekinese
By Trisha Adelena Howell, illustrated by Paul Lopez
32 pages hc 8.5" x 11" ISBN 1-931210-03-9 US $15.95
A princess runs away from her family's new puppy and encounters hard lessons while lost on the streets. When she returns home, her snobbishness is replaced by an appreciation of her blessings. This unusual story with a surprising twist shows the value of love, family, self-examination, and accepting others. Full-color picture book. Ages 4 to adult.

The Pekinese Who Saved Civilization
By Sir Addison Silber Howell, Esq., as told to Trisha Adelena Howell
208 pages sc with 102 b/w photos 5.5" x 8.5" ISBN 1-931210-07-1 US $11.95
You've heard that behind every great man is a great woman, but did you know that behind every great human being is a great dog? Addison the Wonder Dog reveals the true history of the world—from the canine perspective—and humorously shows how to solve all problems, thereby saving civilization. Humor/Social Satire. Ages 8 to adult.

Living In A Glowing World: Poems For Every Season
By Trisha Howell
66 pages sc 5.5" x 8.5" with 9 b/w photos ISBN 1-931210-08-X US $9.95
Each season is an opportunity for beauty, renewal and self-transformation. Through poems tailored to the themes, moods, and emotions of each of the six unique seasons—Winter, Thaw, Spring, Summer, Harvest, and Autumn—this collection of original poetry pleasurably evokes the joys, sorrows, and triumphs of living in a glowing world: a world that is vibrantly alive with energies that can nurture, revitalize, and inspire us all.

Talia and the Tower
By Trisha Adelena Howell, illustrated by David Hohn
288 pages sc with 14 b/w illustrations 5.5" x 8.5" ISBN 1-931210-05-5 US $11.95
Eleven-year-old Talia discovers that the old tower by her family's new home is a portal to ancient worlds and other dimensions of reality. Through a series of six spine-tingling adventures, Talia learns valuable lessons about self-esteem, courage, inspiration, honesty, joy, and self-reliance. Then she and her friends Daniel and Michelle embark on the first of six pulse-racing missions to save the world, traveling to Atlantis to battle the evil Nivid and to save the Great Sapphire of Knowledge. Ages 8 to adult. (1st in a series)

The Journeying Workbook: Adventuring to Unleash Your Inner Power
By Trisha Howell
160 pages sc 8.5" x 11" ISBN 1-931210-06-3 US $12.95
Shamanic journeying—an avenue to the wisdom of the universe through the depths of your being— can be simple and safe for everyone. This powerful practical manual guides you through 100 journeys that can empower your life. You'll learn to reclaim and revitalize all aspects of yourself while benevolent guides lead you through a series of enlightening adventures. From journeying, you can feel more relaxed and happy, and your life can flow effortlessly in harmony with your deepest desires and goals.

The Adventures of Melon and Turnip
By Trisha Adelena Howell, illustrated by Paul Lopez
32 pages hc 8.5" x 11" ISBN 1-931210-04-7 US $15.95
The Adventures of Melon and Turnip follows two friends who venture forth from their garden and make exciting discoveries about life. They encounter an apple tree, a squirrel, a pine tree, a snake, and a grassy field who sing their wisdom through signature songs, enabling Melon and Turnip to discover the value of joy, hard work, honesty, and treating others with love. Full-color picture book. Ages 4 to adult.

NeuroCranial Restructuring: Unleash Your Structural Power, 3rd edition (2001)
By Dean Howell, ND
108 pages sc 5.5" x 8.5" with 22 sets of b/w photos ISBN 1-931210-02-0 US $11.95
A collection of testimonials, articles and answers to frequently asked questions about NeuroCranial Restructuring (NCR), a physical medicine technique that is revolutionizing the treatment of pain and dozens of other conditions. Developed over 21 years by Dr. Howell, NCR creates permanent, incremental improvement in your body's structure. This allows your body to return to its original design: its most vibrant, harmonious, pain-free, and energetic mode of functioning.

NeuroCranial Restructuring: The Ultimate Cranial Therapy (2001 Video)
Produced by Nu Vision Media 110 minutes 1-931210-19-5 US $19.95
This information-packed video features testimonials from 16 patients, explanations about how and why NeuroCranial Restructuring (NCR) treatment works, and a demonstration treatment.

NeuroCranial Restructuring: The Ultimate Cranial Therapy (2001 CD-ROM)
Produced by Nu Vision Media 1-931210-20-9 US $19.95
A CD-Rom featuring instant navigation to each section of the book NeuroCranial Restructuring: Unleash Your Structural Power and of the video NeuroCranial Restructuring: The Ultimate Cranial Therapy.

NeuroCranial Restructuring: The Video (1996)
Produced by Dean Howell, ND 60 minutes US $9.95
This original explanation of NeuroCranial Restructuring (NCR) remains popular because of its low price and its in-depth presentation of the basic concepts of the revolutionary technique.

Coming in 2005:

Talia and the Great Sapphire of Knowledge
By Trisha Adelena Howell, illustrated by David Hohn
128 pages sc with b/w illustrations 5.5" x 8.5" ISBN 1-931210-11-X US $11.95
Twelve-year-old Talia and her friends Daniel and Michelle travel to Egypt, Babylon, Rome, Central America, Elizabethan England, and the United States, encountering great danger and exhilarating adventure as they risk everything to save the Great Sapphire of Knowledge, the repository for all wisdom. Ages 8 to adult. (2nd in a series)

Addie, The Playful Pekingese
By Trisha Adelena Howell, illustrated by David Hohn
128 pages sc with b/w illustrations 5.5" x 8.5" ISBN 1-931210-27-6 US $11.95
Sir Addison the Pekingese is enjoying his retirement—until his rambunctious orphaned niece Addie shows up on his doorstep and turns his life upside down. Funny, dangerous, and poignant adventure follows, involving all the dogs and cats in the neighborhood. This humorous story shows the value of friendship and of community. Ages 8 to adult. (1st in a series)

The Poopy Pekingese
By Trisha Adelena Howell
32 pages hc 8.5" x 11" ISBN 1-931210-09-8 US $15.95
When Addison the Pekingese is forced to attend Kitty's birthday party, he accidentally drinks spoiled milk, and hilarious chaos ensues. This slapstick comedy shows the value of being kind to others. Full-color picture book. Ages 4 to adult.

The Stinky Shepherd
By Trisha Adelena Howell,
32 pages hc 8.5" x 11" ISBN 1-931210-25-X US $15.95
Alex the German Shepherd is so upset about his city's endangered stray dogs that he eats a huge pile of rotting scraps. The resulting noxious gas makes him fly and hilariously enables him to save lives in this slapstick comedy that shows the value of animal companionship and of doing good to others. Full-color picture book. Ages 4 to adult.